Yang the Second and Her Secret Admirers

Yang the Second
and
Her Secret Admirers

Lensey Namioka

Illustrated by Kees de Kiefte

A Yearling Book

Published by
Dell Yearling
an imprint of
Random House Children's Books
a division of Random House, Inc.
1540 Broadway
New York, New York 10036

Visit us on the Web! www.randomhouse.com/kids

Educators and librarians, for a variety of teaching tools, visit us at www.randomhouse.com/teachers

ISBN: 0-440-41641-8

Reprinted by arrangement with Little, Brown & Company

Printed in the United States of America

June 2000

10 9 8 7 6 5 4 3 2

CWO

To Second Sister
— L. N.

For Oskar, Caspar, Daphne, and Ej
— K. de K.

Yang the Second and Her Secret Admirers

1

It was a beautiful catch. I could almost feel the ball smacking into the mitt of the outfielder. The catch put the third batter out, and the side was retired. Our school had won the game!

Actually it wasn't really *my* school. I'm the last boy in the Yang family, and Third Sister and I still go to elementary school. What we were watching was a high school baseball game between a visiting team and the team from Eldest Brother and Second Sister's school.

In our family, I'm the only one who's interested in baseball, and I had to work hard to persuade our family to attend the game. I cheered louder than Eldest Brother and Second Sister, even though it was *their* school that had won.

The outfielder who made that catch was a boy called Paul Eng. I noticed him because he was one of the best players on the team. Besides making that great catch, he had hit a home run in the fifth inning, driving in three runs. I also noticed him because he's Chinese-American.

I wished someone like Paul could be my elder brother. Of course I already have an elder brother, and the two of us get along pretty well. But he has only one interest in life, and that's music. With my terrible ear, I could never become a musician. So Eldest Brother and I have nothing at all in common.

I thought how wonderful it would be if Paul were my brother. He could give me tips on baseball. He could show me how to hit a home run, for instance. I'm not a bad player. In fact my batting average is pretty good. I can tell how the ball is coming at me, and I can usually hit it where I want it to go. But I'm kind of scrawny, and I've never hit a home run in my life. That takes power. I wanted to know how Paul put so much power into his swing.

As we left the stands and squeezed our way to the outside, we found ourselves near the Eng family. We had been introduced to them already at the high school winter concert, so my parents greeted them, and they responded politely.

4

I told the Engs how much I admired Paul's playing. "He drove in three of the four runs!" I crowed. "And his final catch was sensational!"

Father tried to add something. "I admired the way your son . . . er . . . swished his . . . er . . . stick."

"Bat!" I whispered to him. "That stick is called a bat."

"Er . . . yes . . . bat," said Father.

When Paul finally came out of the locker room, his parents and his sister rushed up to congratulate him. I wanted to say something to him, too, but my parents hustled us away to catch the late bus home.

I was still talking about the game when we got back. The others didn't stay around to listen. Father and Eldest Brother went upstairs to go over a violin duet they were practicing. Mother went into the kitchen to cut up more tea bags for breakfast, because she thinks loose tea steeps better. Second Sister said she had to go mend a couple of new holes in her cloth shoes.

"Never mind," said Third Sister, the only one left. "They don't understand baseball, anyway."

From that day on, I began thinking about how I could become a great player like Paul Eng. Was it the way he opened up his arms to swing the bat, or his stance, or the way he ran without looking back after hitting the ball?

Without realizing it, I must have been copying the way Paul moved. Second Sister was the one who noticed it first. "What's wrong with Fourth Brother?" she demanded. "He keeps rotating his arms and shoulders in a peculiar way. It's like watching someone swimming in rice gruel!"

Third Sister is usually on my side, but this time she giggled and said, "And he takes these huge steps. Just the other day, I heard a rip."

I immediately looked down at my pants, to see if my giant steps had ripped the crotch. Third Sister laughed, and I knew she was just teasing me for imitating the way Paul loped along with his long legs.

But with my terrible ear for music, I was used to being laughed at, so I didn't pay much attention to the teasing. Besides, I was too busy thinking of a way to get to know Paul.

My chance finally came one Saturday morning. Money was very tight when we first came to America, but Father is getting more music students and earning good money these days. Also, my sisters make quite a bit from baby-sitting. We even have money left over sometimes for a family treat.

This usually means going to Chinatown on weekends. Mother shops for Chinese groceries, the rest of us browse around in the Oriental shops, and we wind up in a restaurant eating *dim sum*. These are tiny pastries that are steamed, fried, or baked. Some of them are like custards and are sweet, but most are filled with meat, shrimp, and other goodies. We also had *dim sum* in China, but the ones here in Seattle are just as good.

We all love going to a *dim sum* restaurant, because the little dishes of pastries are passed around in carts, and customers just grab whatever they want from a cart. This means you get food in your mouth just seconds after you sit down. For somebody like me who is always hungry, that's very important!

This particular morning, we had to wait in front of the restaurant for Second Sister, who was in a bookstore buying Chinese paperbacks. She spends most of the money she earns on these books. By now we all read English, and when I told her she could save money by going to the public library, she said that for pleasure reading she still preferred Chinese books, because they reminded her of familiar scenes she had left behind.

Once Third Sister said, "Those Chinese books you just bought are adventure stories about outlaws in the olden days. What's familiar about that?"

"At least they're *Chinese* outlaws," retorted Second Sister.

That day I was hungry and getting annoyed at Second Sister for making us all wait. But when she joined us and I saw how tightly she was clutching her bundle of books, I stopped being mad and even began to feel a little sorry for her.

We were finally able to squeeze our way into the crowded *dim sum* restaurant. As we sat down, I recognized the people at the next table. They were the Engs!

A cart came around, and we all made a grab for the dishes there. Paul and I both reached for the same dish of barbecued pork buns. "Hi!" I said to him. "You were great in that game last week."

He was so startled, he let go of the dish, and I got it. "Are you into baseball?" he asked, settling for a dish of pot stickers.

"I play shortstop," I told him, and then added, "I'd give anything to hit a home run. Your home run in the fifth inning went so high, I thought it would sail into Lake Washington!"

My parents exchanged greetings with Mr. and Mrs. Eng, and we all went back to concentrating on the passing carts. One of the carts contained something unfamiliar: big, irregular lumps wrapped in dark green leaves. It seemed to be a new dish the restaurant was trying out. Mr. Eng questioned the waitress pushing the cart.

The exchange was not in English, nor was it in any language I could understand. From their blank expressions, my parents didn't understand, either.

The cart rolled away, and Father asked Mr. Eng what the dish was.

Mr. Eng translated. "Those were dumplings, sticky rice wrapped in giant bamboo leaves. I shouldn't eat them because baking soda is used in preparing the rice, and that's not good for me. I've got high blood pressure, you see."

I was hoping we'd get better acquainted with the Engs. But it didn't work out. A *dim sum* restaurant is not a good place for chatting, because you have to be really alert, or some good food will roll down the aisle before you know it.

"I wonder if we could invite the Engs over one of these days," I said to Third Sister after we got home. "Mother seems awfully lonely sometimes, and so does Second Sister. They could use some friends here in Seattle."

Third Sister and I are close, and she often guesses what's on my mind. "You want Paul to help you with your baseball, don't you?" she asked.

"That, too," I admitted. "Besides, it would be nice to have someone who can give me advice on . . . well . . . all sorts of things boys need advice on."

"On how to shave, for instance?" asked Third Sister.

I saw her dimples, and I knew she was kidding. But I think she understood. I can't imagine consulting either Father or Eldest Brother about anything besides music. And their advice to me would be to stop playing.

Third Sister became thoughtful. "You're

right. About Second Sister being lonely, I mean."

We've been living in America for more than a year now, and Third Sister and I have both made friends. Eldest Brother is a loner, but music is all he cares about, anyway. Second Sister is the one who misses China most, especially the friends she had to leave behind.

"Paul has a sister," I said to Third Sister. "Then Second Sister can become best friends with her, like you and Kim."

Third Sister brought up the subject next evening at dinner. "How about inviting the Eng family to our house for dinner next week?"

"Well, I'll be playing almost every night at the symphony," said Father. That was good news, because at this rate he might become a full-time member of the Seattle Symphony, instead of just a substitute. But it also meant he would be very busy.

Mother also looked doubtful. "How many Engs are there? I saw four of them at least. I don't know . . . I have my hands full just feeding all the Yangs."

Eldest Brother didn't even hear Third Sister's suggestion; he was too busy humming a passage from a piece he'd been practicing.

Second Sister was the worst. She snorted. "Invite the Engs? Whatever for?"

I couldn't very well say, "Because you're lonely and we think you need friends." So I just kept my mouth shut and let Third Sister do all the talking. She's better at it, anyway.

"Well, it would be nice to make friends with a Chinese family," Third Sister suggested.

Second Sister snorted again. Honestly, she was beginning to sound like a horse with a cold. "The Engs can't be a real Chinese family. When we talk to them, we have to speak English!"

We had realized later that Mr. Eng and the waitress had been talking in Cantonese. That's what people speak in Canton, which is in the southern part of China. Our family speaks a form of Mandarin, the dialect spoken by the majority of the people.

"At least they write the same way we do," said Mother. All over China people use the same characters for writing, even though they talk differently.

Second Sister sneered. "Maybe Mr. and Mrs. Eng can write Chinese, but Paul can't. He's in one of my classes, and the other day I heard someone ask him to write his name in Chinese. He said he didn't know how!"

That must have been awfully embarrassing, I thought. One of the first things we learn — even before we go to school — is how to write our name.

"I heard something clever in a Chinese grocery the other day," continued Second Sister. "A young Chinese girl didn't even know what to do with bamboo shoots, and had to ask the clerk! Then an elderly Chinese woman whispered that the girl was a banana: yellow on the outside, but white inside!"

While Second Sister laughed, I finally figured out what she meant: The girl looked Chinese on the outside, but inside she thought just like an American.

"What sort of name is Eng?" asked Third Sister.

"It sounds strange!" said Eldest Brother. "I don't remember ever meeting anybody with that name back in China."

"How do they write it? I wonder," said Mother.

"I asked Mr. Eng, and he wrote it out for me," said Father. He took a scrap of paper from his pocket and wrote down a Chinese character. "This is what he said his name was."

"But we pronounce that name as *Wu!*" cried Mother.

The others all laughed, because the two sounds, *eng* and *wu,* were so different. Second Sister laughed loudest of all. "Eng, eng!" she grunted.

I didn't laugh. I didn't think we were being very nice to the Eng family. Our family is from Shanghai, where the people's accent is a little different from that in Beijing, the capital. But I don't remember visitors from Beijing making fun of us.

When I thought about the way Paul had hit his home run, I thought he deserved better from our family.

Later that night, Third Sister and I went down to the basement, where we played with our cat, Rita. She came streaking in as soon as I scratched out *di-di-di-dah* and *screech!* on my fiddle. She knew that meant a treat, and we didn't disappoint her. I had managed to save a bit of fish from dinner, which I gave to her.

As Rita licked my fingers clean, I said to Third Sister, "I thought Second Sister was awfully mean about the Engs. How would she like it if people made fun of *her* name?"

Third Sister stroked Rita, who made noises like an engine warming up. "No wonder Second Sister can't make friends here," she said. "I feel kind of sorry for her, though."

I didn't feel sorry for Second Sister. I was too busy thinking about how I could hit a home run. The secret was in the swing.

The next day, I happened to glance at Eldest Brother, who was in the living room practicing a fast and loud piece of music. I suddenly realized that he had pretty powerful arms, even if he didn't look all that muscular. Once I had seen him pull himself up to the higher branches of a tall tree to rescue our cat, Rita. Maybe I could get him to teach me how to put power into my swing.

After he had finished practicing and stood wiping his face, I went up to him. "Eldest Brother, do you think you can help me work on my swing?"

He turned around and stared at me. On his face was the expression members of my family always wore whenever they thought I was going to attack a piece of music. It was a mixture of admiration and dread: admiration for my guts, and dread of what they would hear. "Swing?" he said slowly. "Can you tell me the name of the piece?"

I was puzzled. What did he mean by "the piece"? But I kept on. "I want more power in my swing."

"Fourth Brother," Eldest Brother said gravely, "I know you hate to give up music, and you probably think that popular music is much easier to play than classical music."

What was he talking about? "I'm not saying popular music is easy," I protested. "I just want to improve my swing."

"People like Benny Goodman are actually very accomplished musicians," continued Eldest Brother. "You have to understand that if you hope to go into swing."

I gave up. Eldest Brother and I didn't even speak the same language. I had no idea who Benny Goodman was, only that he seemed to be a musician, not a baseball player.

For help in baseball, I needed somebody like Paul Eng. But with Second Sister acting so mean about the Engs, I didn't stand a good chance of getting acquainted with Paul.

For a while things looked pretty hopeless. Then I had my brilliant idea.

2

I got my idea from a movie. Third Sister's best friend, Kim O'Meara, came to our house to play some music with my brother and sisters, and after they finished practicing, Mother invited Kim to stay and eat supper with us.

It's easy to invite a guest at the last minute for a Chinese meal, since all the food is in the middle of the table, and an extra person just means everybody eats a bit less. But Mother always cooks more than enough, anyway, so it's never a problem. Kim eats with us so often that she's become very good with chopsticks.

After supper Kim said her mother had rented a video movie they were going to see. "Would you like to come over and watch it with us, Mary?" she asked Third Sister.

Mary is what Third Sister calls herself when

she's with her American friends. She thinks they have trouble remembering her Chinese name. Most of my friends keep forgetting *my* name, Yingtao, so they call me Sprout. That's because I eat a lot of bean sprouts.

"Sure, I'd love to watch a movie!" Third Sister said eagerly.

We don't often see movies in America, since going to a theater is pretty expensive and we don't have a VCR. In China going to a movie was cheaper, and we also watched a lot of movies on TV. Many of them were from foreign countries — India, Hungary, and countries I'd never heard of — but they were always dubbed into Chinese. For years I thought John Wayne spoke fluent Mandarin.

Kim noticed my wistful expression. "Would you like to come, too, Yingtao?"

"Thanks Kim," I said. I hoped it would be an action picture. "What movie is it?"

"It's called *Much Ado about Nothing*," said Kim. "I'd better warn you that the story is by Shakespeare and he's very old, so some of the people talk a bit funny."

My heart sank. "You mean it's a classic?"

Kim rolled her eyes. "I'm afraid it is. My mom thinks it's good for us to watch a classic."

"I know what you mean," said Third Sister. "My parents are always telling us to read the Chinese classics. At least some of them are fun. I love the stories about the Monkey King. It's full of fights and suspense and kung fu."

"Yeah, well, Mom says this movie has lots of action, too," said Kim. "Besides, Keanu Reeves plays the bad guy in it, and he's cool!"

For a while Kim sat there with a dreamy look on her face. I was even more convinced that the movie wasn't the kind I would enjoy. "Come on, Fourth Brother," said Third Sister. "Why don't we go? It might turn out to be fun."

I finally decided to go watch the movie. If I stayed home, I'd have to listen to Father, Eldest Brother, and several other musicians, who were planning to play an evening of classical music. Either way, I was stuck with the classics.

The movie *was* pretty hard to understand. The funny thing was that after a while, I began to get the hang of the way people talked, and I could sort of follow the story. Mrs. O'Meara had explained the plot before we started, so that helped a lot, too.

The story is about these two characters, Beatrice and Benedick, who dislike each other. Their friends play a trick on them. They make

Beatrice think Benedick is in love with *her*, and they make Benedick think Beatrice is in love with *him*.

These friends know that if they just went and told each one that the other is in love, they wouldn't be believed. So what they do is pretend to be having a secret gossip and arrange to be overheard by both Beatrice and Benedick.

In one scene, the friends make sure Beatrice is eavesdropping, and then say in a loud whisper that Benedick is in love with her. And later they do the same to Benedick. So at the end the two people who disliked each other have changed their minds, because it's hard to dislike someone if you think he or she is in love with you.

Even though I managed to follow the story, I found the movie pretty long, and I was glad when it was finally over. Mrs. O'Meara probably thought we deserved a reward. She put out a big plate of cookies in the kitchen and served each of us a dish of ice cream. After the grown-ups went away, Kim, Third Sister, and I stayed at the kitchen table to work on the cookies.

I was on my third chocolate chip cookie when the idea hit me. *Pow!* I opened my mouth, took a deep breath, and almost choked on my cookie.

Kim brought me a glass of water and pounded me on the back. "Are you okay?"

In my excitement, my tongue practically tripped over itself. "Listen," I croaked, "I just got a wonderful idea! If those people in the movie did it to Beatrice and Benedick, then we could do it to Second Sister and Paul Eng!"

Third Sister blinked. She stared at me silently for a minute, and suddenly her dimples appeared. "Fourth Brother, you're a genius!"

"Who is this Paul Eng?" asked Kim. "Why do

you want to pull a Beatrice-Benedick trick on him?"

It took us a while to explain. First of all, Kim didn't know that there were different kinds of Chinese. "We're so different, we don't even talk the same language," I told her. "We have to use English when we speak to Paul and his family."

"Is that why your sister doesn't like him?" Kim asked, looking surprised. "Just because he has to talk English? Then she must dislike a lot of peo-

ple. In fact that means just about everybody in this country!"

Third Sister tried to explain. "No, it's not that. Second Sister thinks it's okay for *Americans* to speak English . . ."

"Mighty big of her," murmured Kim.

"But she thinks that since Paul is *Chinese*, he ought to be able to speak his own language," finished Third Sister.

"Maybe Paul really thinks that he's an American," said Kim.

Was Paul Chinese, or was he American? He was born in America, and he behaved just like an American. But he ate with chopsticks, and his family went to Chinatown for *dim sum*. He sure looked Chinese. Even if he stayed in this country for a million years, he would still look as Chinese as I do.

"You know, your sister doesn't have any friends here, and she must feel awfully lonely," Kim said slowly. "Wouldn't it be romantic to fix her up with a boyfriend?"

Third Sister broke into a smile. "Okay, let's do it!"

"How are we going to work it?" asked Kim. "Who's going to be overheard by your sister, first of all?"

"It'll have to be me and my brother," Third Sister said. She turned to me. "When shall we start?"

"How about while we're doing the dishes tomorrow night?" I said. "We can start our act as soon as we see Second Sister in the pantry. She always fixes herself a snack before she starts practicing her viola."

"How are we going to get ourselves overheard by Paul?" asked Kim.

"That's the hard part," said Third Sister. "The trouble is, we don't know him very well."

"Jason is in some of Paul's classes," said Kim. "Maybe he can help."

Jason was Kim's elder brother, and he went to the same high school as Paul and Second Sister. "I don't want to bring Jason into this," said Third Sister. "He wouldn't want to get mixed up with a bunch of younger kids, anyway."

"You're right," sighed Kim. "Anyway, his mind is absolutely and totally concentrated on soccer."

We couldn't come up with a good plan to get Paul to overhear a conversation about Second Sister. We sat munching on more cookies and tried to work out what we should say in our make-believe conversation.

"Do you remember what the people in the movie said?" I asked Kim. "I had a hard time following them."

Kim sighed. "So did I. We can't talk like them, anyway. People will think that we're acting — or crazy — or both. We'll have to make up our own conversation."

"You have to be one of the people doing the talking," Third Sister told Kim. "Fourth Brother and I always talk Chinese when we're by ourselves, and Paul won't be able to understand us."

In our family, we still speak Chinese to one another, although more and more English is showing up in our conversations. Third Sister, especially, is always eager to use the English words and phrases in her little notebook.

Kim began to look excited by my idea, too. "All right. What shall I say?"

"Our best bet is to say something about sports," said Third Sister. "You can mention how much Second Sister admired the way he played in that game last week."

"Let's see now . . . how about something like this? . . ." murmured Kim.

Just then I heard the sound of the front door opening. But I was so wrapped up in our make-believe that I didn't pay much attention. Neither did Kim and Third Sister, who were working out their lines.

Kim began. "Boy, your sister was sure impressed by the way he played in that game!"

"Yeah, and she isn't usually interested in American sports," added Third Sister. She sounded quite convincing.

I got into the act, too. "And I thought she didn't even like him! I thought she only liked boys who speak Chinese."

"That's what I thought, too," said Third Sister. "Second Sister told me what really changed her mind was how good he is in math. He's in her math class, you know."

"But I thought he's in the same grade as your eldest brother," said Kim.

"He is," said Third Sister. "But Second Sister is a year ahead in math."

All of us Yang kids are doing really well in our math classes because we've had a head start from our Chinese schools. Most American students, especially the girls, seem to hate math.

"He sits next to her in their math class," continued Third Sister, "but she's too shy to look straight at him. She sneaks a look when she thinks he doesn't notice."

By now I wasn't sure anymore what was true and what was make-believe. I did know, though, that Paul really *was* in Second Sister's math class. The only good thing she ever said about him was that he was one of the top students in the class.

We were beginning to get into the spirit of the thing. "Should we tell him your sister likes him?" said Kim.

"Second Sister would be awfully embarrassed," said Third Sister.

"Well, he's bound to find out," said Kim, laughing. "Sooner or later a boy notices when a girl really likes him."

While we were stopping for breath, we heard steps from the hallway. The steps then went very softly up the stairs.

"Who was that?" asked Third Sister, alarmed.

"Don't worry, that was probably just Jason," said Kim. "He usually gets home around now."

Third Sister got up. "Speaking of getting home, we'd better go. It's late."

"Thanks for letting me watch the movie, Kim," I said, getting up, too. "And thank your mom for the cookies. I'm afraid I ate up all the chocolate chip ones."

"That's okay, Jason doesn't like them much," said Kim. She frowned. "That's funny: Jason always comes into the kitchen first thing after he gets home. I wonder why he sneaked up the stairs like that? It's not like him at all."

I forgot about Jason as I walked home from the O'Mearas'. I was busy planning what Third Sister and I should say the following night as we did the dishes.

3

By the next day I was beginning to have second thoughts about our plot. It could turn out to be really embarrassing for Second Sister.

She looked so unhappy sometimes that I thought it might be mean to play a trick on her. Once, Second Sister, Third Sister, and I were at a shopping mall, and we went into a McDonald's for refreshments (Second Sister agreed to go because there are McDonald's restaurants in China, too). Third Sister saw some of her friends there, and she went over to their table. Soon we heard them talking and laughing.

Second Sister sat with her head down, sipping her Coke, and she suddenly looked very forlorn. In China she had lots of friends, and she would be sitting with them, talking and laughing. She could have made friends here, too, but she preferred to stay home like a grouch.

But Second Sister isn't always a grouch, and I remembered the times when she was kind to me. Like the days when my family still wanted me to play the violin, for instance. Father, Mother, and Eldest Brother had all thought that I played so badly because I wasn't trying hard enough. Second Sister wasn't like the rest of them. She thought that I had it in me to be a good musician, but that I gave up playing so that my friend Matthew could play in our family string quartet. We all knew that Matthew had real musical talent. Second Sister thought I was being noble and letting Matthew take my place because of our friendship. It was just the kind of thing she would do for her own friends. She simply refused to believe that a member of the Yang family would have a terrible ear. It wasn't in our genes.

I wanted to get Third Sister alone and discuss whether we should go on with our trick. But I didn't get a chance. Third Sister came home just before dinner, and we all sat down around the dinner table. Mother had cooked my favorite dish: pork stewed with yellow turnips.

Normally I eat so much of this dish that I get scolded for hogging it (can you hog a dish of pork?).

But I was too busy with my thoughts to eat much. I jumped when Mother said, "What's the matter, Yingtao? Aren't you feeling well? You aren't eating your favorite."

"I'm fine," I muttered. Hurriedly, I took a big helping.

Eldest Brother began to ask Second Sister about the demonstration she had given that day in school. Her class was studying different types of entertainment in countries all over the world, and she had offered to talk about Chinese opera.

To demonstrate background music in opera, Second Sister brought in an *erhu*, a kind of Chinese violin with two strings, and played it to her class. She usually played a viola, but she jumped at this chance to show how a traditional Chinese instrument sounded.

Father beamed. "I'm glad you did it. We concentrate so hard on playing Western music that sometimes we forget there is a long tradition of music in China."

"Did the class enjoy your demonstration?" asked Eldest Brother.

"A few of the kids made faces when I hit the high notes on the *erhu*," said Second Sister. "But most were very interested. Afterward some of them came up and wanted to try it."

Then she frowned. "You know that boy Paul Eng? He told me he had never seen or heard the instrument before!"

I had to defend Paul. "What's so strange about that? I bet very few people in this country have seen one!"

Second Sister's lips curled scornfully. "Maybe that's true of your average American. But you'd think somebody like Paul Eng would care more about his Chinese heritage!"

Lately Second Sister has been using the word *heritage* a lot. I'm not quite sure what she means by our Chinese heritage. Does she mean being as Chinese as possible? But her own instrument is a viola, a Western instrument. Or does she mean clothes? Is that why she likes to wear her cloth jacket with the high collar and buttons down the front? Maybe she means eating Chinese food with chopsticks. But Paul ate Chinese food — the whole Eng family had been eating *dim sum* in Chinatown just the other day.

Listening to the scornful way Second Sister talked about Paul, I decided it would be a great joke after all to get the two of them together, like that couple in the movie. My eyes met Third Sister's, and we nodded to each other.

In our family Third Sister and I do the dishes, while Second Sister and Eldest Brother help Mother with some of the cooking. As Third Sister scraped the garbage into the disposal, I filled a big pan with hot, sudsy water and began putting the dishes in.

The chopsticks I washed by rubbing them against one another: You hold a bunch of them and roll them between your two hands, making a *burrrr* sound. The rubbing makes the chopsticks really clean.

Once I even did it in time to music. Eldest Brother was practicing a piece, and I added a rhythmic part with the chopsticks. I have a terrible ear for pitch — that is, I'm no good at telling high from low. But I've got pretty good rhythm. Eldest Brother enjoyed my chopsticks accompaniment. It was the only time he ever said anything good about my music making.

"Shh! Not so loud with the chopsticks," whispered Third Sister. "I think Second Sister is finished in the pantry. Let's start when she goes up the stairs."

I dropped the chopsticks into the pan, and after a minute Third Sister winked at me in a signal to begin our act.

"Isn't it touching," said Third Sister in a loud whisper, "the way Paul Eng went up to Second Sister after her demonstration?"

This wasn't the opening line we had planned, but it was a good one. I did my best to play up to it. "Yeah, he must have been really hurt when she didn't say anything friendly back to him."

We paused and listened. Second Sister's steps paused at the foot of the stairs. Instead of going up to her room to practice, she was stopping to hear more.

"Are you sure he likes her?" asked Third Sister. Now we were using the lines we had rehearsed. "After all, she hasn't been nice to him at all. In fact she's been awfully mean every time his name comes up."

There was no sound from Second Sister. She must have been listening intently. I risked a short pause, and washed a few plates. Then I sighed heavily. "Poor Paul. I asked him once about his batting stance. He was very nice to me

and explained everything patiently." I paused to wash a couple of rice bowls before continuing. "Then he looked at me sort of anxiously. He asked me whether Second Sister ever went out with boys — you know, on dates."

"So that *proves* he likes her!" exclaimed Third Sister. "What did you tell him?"

"I had to tell him the truth," I said, and sighed again. "I told him Second Sister wouldn't look at a boy who didn't speak Chinese."

"Poor Paul!" Third Sister said. The two of us were beginning to repeat ourselves, so we didn't say anything more and went on washing dishes. Besides, we had said enough.

Our ears were eagerly cocked, and sure enough, we could hear Second Sister's steps going slowly up the stairs. They sounded thoughtful.

Arranging for Paul to overhear Kim and Third Sister wasn't easy. The trouble was that neither our family nor the O'Mearas knew the Engs outside of school. Besides, Third Sister, Kim, and I went to elementary school, while Paul went to the same high school as Eldest Brother and Second Sister. Except at school concerts or baseball games, we just didn't run into the Engs much.

Days passed, and I almost gave up hope. I noticed that Second Sister sometimes had on a peculiar expression. Her face would be screwed up, like she was trying to get a piece of gristle out from between her teeth. She must have been chewing over our remarks she had overheard.

That meant the first part of our scheme was working. But what good did it do if we couldn't carry out the second part?

Our chance came at last. It was our spring vacation, and as a treat Mrs. O'Meara took Kim, Third Sister, and me to visit the Pacific Science Center.

Mrs. O'Meara said she was sick and tired of having kids underfoot all the time. "Jason is acting really strange," she said. "He goes around mooning and bumping into things!" So she chased him out of the house with orders to practice soccer with his friends. It was the first time she ever had to order him to practice.

Mrs. O'Meara offered to drop Kim and Third Sister at the Science Center. I had hoped to play with my friend Matthew, but he had to go to the dentist. He protested that it was totally unfair for someone to see a dentist during vacation. "Life *is* totally unfair," said his mother as she dragged him off.

So Mrs. O'Meara took me along with Kim and Third Sister, who didn't mind me tagging along. It turned out to be a good thing we went together.

The Science Center is a big museum with lots of buttons to push. Things go squirting and squeaking and beeping and gurgling. We're supposed to learn important scientific facts from all this. In spite of that, it's loads of fun.

While Kim and Third Sister played with machines that speeded up their voices and made them sound like Donald Duck, I went over to look at a box containing poisonous spiders. Next to that was a tall glass case with a section of a beehive in it. I was just about to go over when I saw Paul Eng standing behind the case, looking at the bees.

I rushed over to Third Sister and grabbed her arm. "I saw Paul over there!" I whispered. "Come on! This is our chance to carry out our plan!"

Third Sister and I hurried over to the case of bees, and she began her speech. Then she stopped. Kim had to be in the act, too, and she was still back at the sound machine, making like Donald Duck!

We ran back and got Kim over, but by then Paul had already gone.

Looking around frantically, we spotted him going into the dinosaur exhibit room. He stopped and peered at a tyrannosaurus, which roared menacingly.

We quickly positioned ourselves behind the dinosaur. Third Sister and Kim opened their mouths and tried to start our script.

ROAR, went the tyrannosaurus. The three of us looked at one another and shook our heads. This wasn't going to work.

I waited until I saw Paul reach one of the quiet dinosaurs, an armored stegosaurus. There was no time to be lost. "Come on!" I hissed to the other two.

Again we got ourselves into position, and Kim cleared her throat. "So what makes you think your sister likes Paul Eng?" she asked.

"Well, she was impressed by the way he played in that ball game," said Third Sister, "and she isn't usually interested in American sports."

I came in with my lines. "And I thought she

didn't like him! I thought she only liked boys who spoke Chinese."

"That's what I thought, too," said Third Sister. "Second Sister told me what really changed her mind was how good he is in math. He's in her math class, you know."

As I listened to our act, the lines suddenly sounded really stiff and unnatural. How could anyone believe something as lame as this?

Maybe Kim and Third Sister felt that way, too. Their voices petered out and stopped. Then without another word, we began to shuffle off. I didn't dare to look behind me at Paul to see how he had taken our words.

We went to the food court, where we were supposed to wait for Mrs. O'Meara to pick us up. For a while the three of us sipped our drinks without saying anything. I broke the silence and got the last drop of my drink with a loud slurp. "Do you think he fell for the act?"

"I don't know," muttered Kim. "It was okay when we were practicing the other day, but it sounded awfully phony just now."

Third Sister and I nodded. We both knew what she meant. In a way, I was almost relieved.

Suddenly Third Sister grabbed my arm. "Isn't that him over there?" she hissed.

She was right. Paul was standing at the pie counter, buying some refreshments. He was also buying something for his companion, the girl standing next to him.

It seemed that we had been wasting our time: Paul already had a girlfriend!

4

I felt a kick on my leg from Third Sister. She had seen Paul's girlfriend, too. I nodded and pointed out the couple to Kim.

The three of us sighed in unison. "I'm sorry," I said. "I should have found out whether Paul already had a girlfriend before we started all this."

We sat around glumly and thought about all the time and energy we had wasted. Then I heard a step behind me, and a soft cough.

"Hello," said Paul Eng's voice.

I spun around and stared. Paul and his girlfriend were standing by our table.

"Hi, Paul," I said weakly. Then I said the first thing that came into my head, "I'd give anything to hit a home run!"

Third Sister had better manners. "Hi, I don't

know if you remember me. I'm Mary, and this is my friend Kim."

Paul looked embarrassed. That wasn't surprising, after the conversation he had overheard. In his place, I would have avoided the Yang family like chicken pox.

But for some strange reason, Paul didn't go away. He just stood there. Three months seemed to go by as we all waited and squirmed.

Finally the girl with Paul poked him. He cleared his throat, swallowed, and said, "This is my sister, Melanie. You met her at the *dim sum*, restaurant, didn't you?"

Now I realized that the girl looked familiar. She wasn't his girlfriend at all. She was his sister! There was still hope our trick might work.

Melanie poked her brother again, and again Paul cleared his throat. "You have another sister, don't you? Her name is Yinglan, right?" His voice sort of died off.

Third Sister and I nodded solemnly. "That's right," I acknowledged. "I do have another sister, called Yinglan."

There was a pause. The five of us stared at one another some more, and three more months passed.

It's hard for Americans to remember Chinese

names. Unlike Third Sister, Second Sister refused to give herself an English name. I thought it was a good sign that Paul knew Second Sister's name, since that meant he had really paid attention to her — even before we played our trick.

Melanie poked Paul for the third time, and for the third time he cleared his throat. A family of frogs must have set up housekeeping with his tonsils. "Er . . . I noticed Yinglan in my math class," he began. "But she's only a sophomore, isn't she?"

"She got put a year ahead," admitted Third Sister. Then she added quickly, "It's not that she's a math genius, or anything. It's just that Chinese schools are more advanced in math."

"Very good, very good . . . ," said Paul absently. Then he must have realized that he sounded foolish, and his voice faded. Suddenly he took a deep breath and said in a rush, "Does your sister ever go out with boys, you know, on dates?"

We did it! Our trick had worked! I caught Third Sister's eye, and we both smothered an urge to laugh. Paul's words were almost exactly the same as the ones Second Sister had overheard while we were doing dishes!

Paul must have seen the laughter in our eyes.

He turned red as a sunset. Dragging Melanie after him, he rushed out of the food court. He almost crashed into Mrs. O'Meara, who had come to pick us up.

"Who was that?" asked Mrs. O'Meara, staring after the Engs. "Friends of yours?"

"I hope so," Third Sister said slowly. She looked at me and then at Kim. The three of us beamed at one another and silently congratulated ourselves on our success.

The dinner table that night was very quiet. Father was out of town, playing with the Seattle Symphony, which was on tour.

Third Sister and I spent all our time stealing glances at Second Sister. She was eating slowly, very slowly. She picked up each grain of rice in her bowl with her chopsticks, looked it over absently, and then brought it up to her mouth.

As usual, Eldest Brother was thinking about some piece of music. He tapped the table with his left hand occasionally, trying out some fingering.

Suddenly Mother broke the silence. "What's the matter with everybody? You've all swallowed your tongues!" She glared at Second

Sister. "You're the worst, Yinglan! In fact you've been acting really bizarre all week!"

"Did something happen to you in school?" Third Sister asked innocently.

But Second Sister only shook her head, blushed a little, and went back to eating her grains of rice one by one.

The phone rang in the kitchen, and Mother went to answer it. "For you, Yingmei," she told

Third Sister when she came back to the table. "It's your friend Kim."

When Third Sister came back after talking on the phone, she was frowning. I wondered if the call had something to do with the trick we were playing.

After dinner, Third Sister hurried me into the kitchen, where we started to do the dishes again. "We've got to go over to the O'Mearas'," she whispered.

"What happened?" I asked.

"Kim said it's an emergency," Third Sister whispered. She stopped, because we heard Second Sister's steps at the foot of the staircase. The steps paused. No question about it, Second Sister was hoping to eavesdrop some more.

But this time we definitely did not want to be overheard. We silently went on washing dishes. After a couple of minutes, Second Sister apparently gave up hope of hearing anything interesting. We heard her footsteps slowly going up the stairs.

After we finished the dishes, we told Mother that we were going to the O'Mearas'. For Third Sister to visit Kim was pretty normal, since they'd been best friends for months. Mother was a bit surprised to see me tagging along.

"The O'Mearas rented a movie I'm interested in," I muttered.

"What, again?" said Mother. "It's getting embarrassing, how often you go to the O'Mearas' to watch movies."

I didn't enjoy lying to Mother, although I was telling the literal truth, since everything had started from that movie about — what are their names? — Beatrice and Benedick. But I *felt* like a liar because I was trying to mislead Mother. The trouble with lying is that you always sink in deeper and deeper, and you're sorry you ever started it.

When Kim opened the front door, she put her finger to her lips for silence. Her parents and Jason were watching TV in the living room, but Kim hurried us up the stairs. Once in her room, she closed the door carefully.

"What's the great mystery?" asked Third Sister. I had a feeling of doom.

I was right. Kim took a deep breath. "It's Jason. He thinks your sister has a crush on him!"

We goggled at her. Finally I found my voice, and what I found was a thin squeak. "Are you sure?"

"What makes you think so, Kim?" asked

Third Sister. Her voice sounded as squeaky as mine.

"It came out at supper tonight," said Kim. "Jason said his soccer team was playing next week. He asked Dad and Mom if they could take your sister to the game, since she would probably like to go."

Expecting Second Sister to watch Jason play soccer was like expecting Mother to swoon over Elvis Presley. Third Sister and I goggled some more. Again I said, "Are you sure?"

Kim nodded. "Jason is awfully bashful around girls, and he never talks about them at home because he's afraid we'll tease him. But tonight, right out of the blue, he claimed your sister liked him."

Third Sister took a deep breath. "That's absolutely —" She hurriedly consulted her little book of English phrases for something strong. It didn't help. "What exactly did Jason say?" she finally asked.

Kim frowned, trying to remember. "Well, he said that your sister was sure impressed by the way he played soccer."

"But Second Sister has never seen Jason play!" objected Third Sister.

"What else did he say?" I asked.

"Let's see," said Kim. "Yeah, he said your sister sat next to him in math class, and she was too shy to look straight at him, but she would steal a look at him when she thought he didn't notice."

"You know, there's something awfully familiar about those words," muttered Third Sister. "Where have I heard them before?"

Then the realization hit all three of us. "Those are exactly the words we were rehearsing!" I cried.

"Jason must have overheard us when we were practicing here that day!" Kim said.

Suddenly I remembered the sound of Jason's footsteps going up the stairs while we were talking in the kitchen. They were the soft, careful steps of someone who had received a shock, someone who had a lot to think about.

So why was Jason shocked? Third Sister answered the question. "Jason must have thought we meant *him!*" she breathed.

Kim smacked herself on the forehead. I had seen it done in movies and comic strips, but this was the first time I saw it in real life. "Oh, my God!" she cried. "When we talked about your sister being impressed by the way he played in that game, Jason thought we were talking about *him* playing in a *soccer* game!"

"I bet that's what happened," Third Sister said slowly. "We never actually mentioned Paul Eng by name."

I went over our pretend conversation word for word. "That's right. And we didn't say baseball. We only talked about a ball game. So Jason thought we meant a soccer game and *he* was the one she admired so much!"

Suddenly Kim went into a fit of giggles. I felt my insides wobbling violently, and a *yak* exploded out of me. Third Sister began to rock herself back and forth, and had trouble catching her breath.

We finally sobered up when we began to think about the fallout.

"What should we do?" asked Kim. "We can't let Jason go around thinking your sister has a crush on him!"

"What about your parents?" asked Third Sister. "Do they feel funny about the idea of a Chinese girl falling for Jason?"

Kim rolled her eyes and thought for a while. "I don't think they're upset about the Chinese part," she said finally. "After all, *we*'re friends and they're happy about that."

That was true. The O'Mearas had always made us feel welcome in their home.

"My parents were just a little surprised," continued Kim. "Your sister is always standoffish, you know? So my folks were kind of tickled by the whole thing."

"I guess we'd better go and straighten Jason out about the misunderstanding," Third Sister said heavily. She wasn't very enthusiastic.

Neither was I. I used to think Jason was nasty because he called Eldest Brother a nerd for being interested only in music and not in sports. That was before he had seen Eldest Brother climb a tall tree to rescue our kitten, Rita. After that Jason had become much more pleasant.

Although I didn't really dislike Jason anymore, I had to admit I rather liked the idea of playing a trick on him. Third Sister felt the same way. "Do we really have to do anything?" she asked. Her dimples twinkled.

5

When we came home from school the next day, Mother had a surprised look on her face. "The O'Mearas are inviting you kids to go with them this Saturday to watch Jason play in a sock-her game," she said.

We speak Chinese at home, and what Mother had said sounded like Jason was playing a game where he went around punching people, especially girls. We finally got straightened out: When Mrs. O'Meara mentioned "soccer," Mother had thought she said "sock-her."

Since we knew about Jason's misunderstanding, the news wasn't unexpected. Third Sister tried to look puzzled. "Why me? I don't know anything at all about soccer!"

Mother shook her head. "They're inviting not only you and Yingtao, but also Yinglan!"

Second Sister stared in complete disbelief when she was told about the invitation. "Why on earth would I want to go to a sock-her game? It sounds brutal and utterly idiotic! Maybe the O'Mearas mean Eldest Brother, although I can't imagine why he would want to go, either."

"No, they definitely said something about my two daughters," said Mother. "But if you don't want to go, you'd better call them and tell them so."

As Second Sister went off to phone the O'Mearas, Mother added, "Try to be polite about it, Yinglan."

"I'm always polite," growled Second Sister.

"And don't growl," said Mother.

Apparently Second Sister listened to Mother's warning, because we heard her voice sounding soft and pleasant as she called up the O'Mearas. After she had hung up, she returned to the kitchen looking dazed.

"So you told them you can't go?" I asked.

"I said I'd go," muttered Second Sister. "Mrs. O'Meara said that Jason particularly asked for me."

Leaving Mother and Second Sister staring at each other, Third Sister and I rushed upstairs to my room. We had to get away before we burst.

As soon as I closed the door to my room, we both collapsed laughing.

"We w-wanted S-Second Sister interested in a b-ballplayer," sputtered Third Sister. "But it's the wrong b-ball and the wrong player!"

I stopped laughing before she did. I really wanted Second Sister friendly with Paul because of baseball. Instead, we had ended up with Jason and soccer.

Second Sister can be very cutting at times. Maybe she'd say something sarcastic about the game on Saturday, and it would make Jason so mad that he'd back off. Once he was out of the way, we could go back to our plot involving Paul.

By now we should have known that things didn't always turn out the way we planned.

Jason drove some of his teammates to the playing field, while Mrs. O'Meara took us and Kim. On the way over, Kim explained soccer to us. "Each team has eleven players. You're not allowed to touch the ball with your hands, and the only way to move it is to kick it or bounce it with your head or chest. The aim is to get the ball into your opponents' goal."

"Why do you people call this game sock-her?" exclaimed Second Sister. "It's just football!"

Kim looked mystified. "What are you talking about? This isn't football. It's soccer!"

Third Sister, our family expert on everything American, managed to straighten them out. "In China we call soccer football," she told Kim. Then she turned to Second Sister. "Americans call football soccer, and it's spelled *s-o-c-c-e-r*, not 'sock-her.' "

"Why don't Americans call the game football?" muttered Second Sister. "It's played with the foot, after all!"

I usually disagree with Second Sister when she picks on Americans. But this time she had a point. The foot isn't used in American football, except for kicking a field goal.

The previous fall I had watched some American football games on TV with my friend Matthew. The players were so huge that they didn't even look human. They wore armor and helmets, and they spent their time crashing violently into each other. Seattle is a city that's mad about football. So I tried my best to understand the game, and Matthew did his best to explain. But it was hard going. We finally agreed that we both liked baseball more. Another reason I prefer baseball is because you don't have to be huge to be a good player.

In addition to football — American football, that is — and baseball, people in Seattle are also big on basketball. There is a lot less interest in professional soccer.

But in China soccer is very popular. Many schools, factories, and cities have teams. I had gone to a few games in China, but I never became a soccer expert. I found it confusing. All the players, except the goalkeepers, were constantly milling about, so you couldn't tell who was doing what. It's not like baseball, where the players stand in their proper places and the action comes in sharp spurts.

Today I could at least tell the teams apart by the colors of the players' shirts. Jason's team wore green, and the opposing team wore black shirts with yellow stripes.

In our family, Second Sister was the football — I mean soccer — fan. Back in China she used to go to games with her friends, and she became quite an expert.

We had no trouble finding seats in the stands. Mrs. O'Meara sat with Second Sister, while Third Sister, Kim, and I sat in the row in front of them. Listening to the other spectators, I decided that we Yangs were probably the only people who were not relatives of the players.

"Hi, Karen!" Mrs. O'Meara called to a friend of hers. "I see Kevin's knee is much better." The various soccer mothers exchanged greetings. I hunched myself inside my jacket and expected a chilly and boring afternoon in front of me.

Things changed after the kickoff. Second Sister began to pay close attention, and her face lost its usual sour expression. Looking over the field, she began to comment on the plays. "Why are those boys all bunched up over there?" she complained. "They should spread out more."

For a while things didn't go well for Jason's team. "They should watch that right side," Second Sister muttered. "The boy standing near the dividing line . . . What's he called?"

"You mean the midfielder?" said Mrs. O'Meara. She seemed a little surprised at Second Sister's expertise.

"That's the one," said Second Sister. "He's looking in the wrong direction!" Suddenly she screeched. "Hey, look out!" In her excitement she had yelled in Chinese.

Startled, I swiveled around to look at her. My

jacket was too big, since it was meant to last several seasons. I had so much room inside it that when I turned, it remained facing front. Mrs. O'Meara and her friend screamed. I realized that to them, my head seemed to be screwed on backward.

With Second Sister yelling in Chinese and the soccer moms behind us screaming, it was noisier

in our part of the stands than among the players. Then everyone's attention went back to the field, because something exciting was happening there.

Jason's team had the ball at last, but before they could move it toward the other team's goal, they lost control of it again. There were groans all around us. One of the loudest groans came from Second Sister.

A member of the yellow-striped team got the ball and was nudging it along with little kicks, using the side of his foot. The players in green danced around him, trying to get the ball away. But some member of the yellow-striped team

always got in the way and managed to keep the green team from getting at the ball. The ball was being worked closer and closer to the green team's goal.

Suddenly one of the green players slid to the ground and kicked at the ball between the legs of the yellow-striped player. It was Jason! He kicked the ball away from the enemy and into the path of one of his own team.

We all jumped up and cheered. We cheered even louder when a player in green kicked the ball into the goal. The score was now 1–0, in favor of Jason's team.

Second Sister cheered loudest of all. Looking at her shining face, I realized that I hadn't seen her so excited since we left China.

That goal for the green team turned out to be the only score in the game, and Jason's team won. This put all of us in a good mood. When Jason came over after the game, we congratulated him heartily.

"That slide tackle of yours was pretty good," Second Sister told Jason.

"It was an awful mess in there," mumbled Jason bashfully. "I'm surprised you could make anything out."

"Your footwork was great," Second Sister

complimented him. It didn't sound like flattery, either.

Jason still looked bashful, but he was obviously very pleased. "I'm surprised you know so much about soccer. Most people here think the game is kind of sissy. It's only beginning to be popular, but we have a long way to go before we catch up with baseball, football, or basketball."

"Soccer is very popular in China," Second Sister told him. "I used to go to a lot of the games."

Jason beamed. "You did? Say, would you like to go to our next game? It's two weeks from Saturday."

Second Sister suddenly looked shy. "Well, I don't know. I'll have to see what my schedule is . . ."

Mrs. O'Meara came to her rescue. "It's getting chilly, and we'd better not stand around talking. I'll take Kim and the Yangs home." She turned to Jason. "You're driving your friends back, aren't you?"

"Uh . . . not exactly," said Jason. "The others are going back separately." Suddenly he looked up at Second Sister and said in a rush, "Can I take you back, Yinglan?"

We were all stunned by surprise — Jason most of all, apparently.

As we stood there like statues, a couple of people tried to move past us to the exit. "Oh, hi there!" said one of them. The voice was kind of familiar.

I looked around and saw that it was Melanie Eng. Did that mean Paul played soccer, as well as baseball? I hadn't seen him among the players.

"I came to see Amy's brother play," explained Melanie, indicating a friend nearby. So we weren't the only nonrelatives at the game. "I didn't know you liked soccer," she said, looking around at us.

Second Sister stirred and pulled herself together. "I — uh — I didn't realize that sock-her was really soccer — I mean — football was just soccer — I mean — soccer was just football."

She was gibbering and she knew it. Turning to Mrs. O'Meara, she said, "I'd better go home with Yingmei and Yingtao, after all. I still have some homework and practicing to do."

Father and Mother greeted us when we got home.

"Well, how did you enjoy the game?" Mother asked casually.

Although the question was addressed to all of us, it was clear that Mother was asking Second Sister.

"I had a good time," said Second Sister, sounding almost surprised. "It was a football game, you know. I haven't seen football since I left China, and it was good to go to a game again."

This was a change from Second Sister's usual nasty cracks about anything American. The pleasant expression on her face was a nice change, too.

Third Sister and I went down to the basement. That was our place for playing with our kitten and having a private chat.

As usual I scratched the notes on my violin that meant a treat, and a minute later Rita came streaking in to eat the bit of meatball I had saved for her.

I stroked Rita. "Things aren't turning out quite the way we planned, Third Sister. What should we do?"

"Do we have to do anything?" asked Third Sister. "Why don't we just wait and see what happens next?"

I thought about Second Sister's happy face during the game. "Yes, but Second Sister might wind up going out with Jason! I thought our whole purpose was to get her together with Paul!"

"That's not true," said Third Sister. "I wanted Second Sister to make friends with somebody because she was so lonely. You only wanted to get acquainted with Paul so you could get help with baseball."

"Yes, but we've already got Paul and Second Sister thinking that they like each other," I objected.

"I guess you're right," admitted Third Sister. "Now that we got the ball rolling, we can't just leave them dangling like this."

Third Sister likes to practice the English phrases in her notebook, even when she's speaking Chinese. Sometimes she mixes the expressions together. I pictured Paul and Second Sister dangling over a rolling ball.

"We've got to do something," I said. "It's getting out of hand!" Now *I* was doing it: I could see the ball — a baseball, of course, not a soccer ball — rolling out of our hands.

"Maybe we should confess," said Third Sister. "That would be a load off our minds and let us off the hook." At this rate, she would use up her whole list of English expressions.

Frankly I wasn't eager to confess our plot. "When Second Sister gets mad, she can be awfully scary," I reminded her.

"All right," sighed Third Sister. "We'll just have to wait and see what happens next."

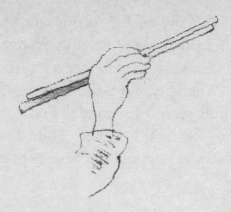

6

Two days later when I came home from school, I saw Mother hanging up the phone. "That's funny," she murmured.

"What's funny?" I asked, wondering if it was fallout from our plotting.

It *was*, but not what I had expected. "The Engs are inviting our family for dinner," said Mother.

"That's great!" I cried before I could stop myself.

"But we don't know the Engs that well," said Mother, looking a little startled by my enthusiasm. "We've only met them a few times."

"Then this is our chance to know them better!" I declared.

"I'll have to see if your father is free," said Mother.

When Father came home that night, she told him about the invitation. "Do you think we should accept?" Mother asked.

"Why not?" said Father. To my delight, he repeated my words. "The Engs seem like pleasant people, and I'd like to know them better."

Mother, however, was doubtful about Second Sister. "I have the impression that Yinglan doesn't care for them," she said.

"What makes you think so?" asked Father, looking surprised.

"Every time Paul Eng's name comes up, she says something unpleasant," replied Mother. She paused, then added, "It's too bad, because he seems like a nice boy, and just the right age for Yinglan."

"The right age!" sputtered Father. "They're much too young for your matchmaking!"

"You're right, you're right," Mother said hurriedly. "I was just thinking of the old days, when girls even younger than Yinglan got married. Anyway, she seems more interested in the O'Meara boy, Jason."

Jason was a complication that could spoil everything. "Second Sister only admires Jason because of soccer," I told my parents quickly.

"Well, about the Engs," said Mother, "if Yinglan doesn't like them, she doesn't have to go to their dinner. We can think of some excuse."

When asked if she wanted to go to the Engs, Second Sister surprised Mother by blushing like a pomegranate. She cleared her throat a few times. "If they invited the whole family, then of course I'll have to go. It would be rude not to accept."

I reported to Third Sister after she came home from the O'Mearas', where she and Kim had been doing their homework together.

"Wow," she breathed. "This is exactly what you wanted, isn't it?"

"Let's hope Second Sister doesn't take it into her head to say something mean," I said. But I didn't think she would, not after the way she had blushed. Besides, she could have refused to go as Mother suggested, and she didn't. I really thought our plot was transforming Second Sister from an ogre into a good fairy.

"Kim says Jason was walking on air after the soccer game," Third Sister added. "He thinks Second Sister must be a real soccer fan, and he keeps harping on how much girls admire athletes."

"Is Kim worried about Jason finding out the truth and getting mad at us?" I asked.

Third Sister's dimples twinkled. "She can hardly wait for him to find out. It will take him down a peg, she says."

I had a vision of Jason floating in the air, playing a harp like an angel, and then stepping down on a wooden peg. I felt a twinge of guilt. Jason had been really great in that soccer game. Kicking the ball between the legs of the yellow-striped player had been a tricky shot, and he fully deserved Second Sister's admiration.

I decided not to worry about Jason. The important thing was to make sure that our dinner with the Engs would be the start of a close friendship between our two families.

The next day, Third Sister reported a good sign. It seemed that Second Sister had actually gone to Chinatown and bought herself a pair of shoes! For a long, long time, she had refused to give up the pair of cloth shoes she had brought with her from China. Of course the new pair looked exactly like her old pair: black cotton tops with a strap across the instep, and brown plastic soles. Her old ones she tenderly stored away in the paper box that the new ones came in.

I wondered if Second Sister would get a new dress, too. But that was expecting too much. She still wore her Chinese jacket with the high collar, and her wrists stuck out a couple of inches beyond the cuffs. I was so used to seeing her like this that it didn't bother me, but Third Sister winced.

When Father rang the doorbell to the Engs, Mr. Eng opened the front door and a familiar smell came floating out into our faces. It was a smell of soy sauce, scallions, and ginger. My mouth immediately watered. Whatever else happened, we would have a delicious Chinese meal.

"Come in, come in!" Mr. Eng said heartily.

Paul loomed up just behind his father. He was more than a head taller. But when our family entered the house, he faded back and busied himself examining his shoes.

"Sheila and the girls are in the kitchen," said Mr. Eng, inviting us to sit down. "Would you like something to drink?"

I noticed that when we go to dinner with American families, there would be a stretch — a very long stretch — when the grown-ups drink wine, beer, or even liquor, and talk before eating.

I had been hoping that the Engs, being Chinese, would get to the real food right away. But it seemed that they followed the American custom. Father and Mother each accepted some beer.

Paul busied himself pouring pop for us kids. He spoke in a gruff voice and wouldn't look up at us.

There were little dishes of pretzels, nuts, and potato chips with gooey things to dip them in. I didn't touch the dip, since I knew from experience that my chip usually got stuck in the goo and broke off.

I had nothing against these snacks, but this was a sign that we'd have to wait a while before we'd get to the food producing those wonderful smells from the kitchen.

Mrs. Eng came out and joined us in the living room. "Melanie said she's going to do the stir-fried dishes," she said proudly.

Stir-frying is the trickiest part of cooking a Chinese meal. In fact the cook usually does it while the guests are already seated at the table.

At this hopeful sign, our family promptly got up and started for the dining room. But when we saw that Mr. and Mrs. Eng stayed put on the sofa, we quickly beat a retreat and sank down in our seats again.

If Mrs. Eng was surprised by our move, she didn't mention it. "It's nice of Melanie to do some of the cooking," she said. "This means I

can visit with you before dinner." To my dismay, she seemed prepared for a nice long visit.

While the grown-ups were chatting, I tried to forget about my stomach, which was threatening to complain out loud at any minute. Desperately I grabbed another handful of peanuts. Mother shook her head at me, but I pretended not to see her.

Instead I looked at Second Sister and Paul, who had seated themselves at opposite ends of the room. Every now and then they'd steal a glance at each other. If their eyes happened to meet, both of them would blush. Paul then went back to studying his shoes. After a while Second Sister peered down at her shoes, too.

Nothing exciting was happening between them. I looked around the room, while the grown-ups carried on their conversation. Our living room at home was always messy with music stands, piles of sheet music, and instruments. By comparison the Engs' living room looked incredibly neat.

Hanging on the wall were a couple of black-and-white ink paintings. One showed some rugged mountains with little pine trees on them, and the other one showed stalks of bamboo next to some rocks. Second Sister would approve. She liked ink paintings, and even did some herself. Also, these were *Chinese* paintings. But she wasn't looking at the pictures. She was too busy studying her shoes and stealing glances at Paul.

Aside from the paintings, the living room was like others we had seen in America. The grown-ups sat on a big squashy sofa and two chairs which matched the sofa, while we kids sat on wooden chairs brought in from the dining room.

In fact the furniture looked a bit like the O'Mearas'. I began to wonder whether the Engs were really Chinese or American. Then I realized that I was beginning to think like Second Sister.

At long last, the door to the kitchen opened, and Melanie came out to announce that dinner was served.

I sprang up practically with a *boing*. Even Third Sister didn't try to hold me down. This time we were able to continue our march into the dining room without having to retreat.

To my delight, in the middle of the table were platters full of delectable-looking food. This meant we could take what we liked from the platters. I like this better than American dinners, where I would be served a plate full of stuff I didn't choose. In eating, at least, the Engs were as Chinese as we were.

We didn't need Mrs. Eng's urging to help ourselves. I started to use my chopsticks to pick up a piece of pork from a platter, but I felt a kick from Third Sister. She pointed at the serving spoon on the platter, and I remembered that in America we're supposed to use that instead of poking our own chopsticks into the common dish. Third Sister once explained to me that Americans think it's unsanitary for people to dig into a dish with their own utensils, since that would be sharing germs. (This doesn't stop Americans from shaking hands with strangers, or even — ugh! — kissing them.)

But we forgot our American manners when Melanie came out proudly carrying a dish of stir-fried prawns. They looked so luscious that five pairs of Yang chopsticks were raised instantly to reach out for the prawns. Third Sister was the only one who held back. She gave a warning cough.

At this reminder, the rest of us stopped cold, with our chopsticks still in the air. The whole dinner party froze.

I had an inspiration. Waving my chopsticks like a conductor's baton, I began to hum — at least I tried to hum. "Is this how the last movement went in your concert yesterday?" I asked Father.

Father caught on immediately. "Er . . . yes," he said, and began to wave his chopsticks, too. The other Yangs followed suit, and we all began to hum.

The Engs sat with their mouths open. Finally our humming died away, and Mrs. Eng smiled weakly. "I've heard that your family is musically gifted. Now I see why."

After that I went thankfully back to the food, which tasted every bit as good as it looked. I did remember to use the serving spoons to help myself, however.

"Your prawns are delicious!" Second Sister told Melanie, who was seated next to her. "They're cooked not a second too long."

Melanie looked very pleased. "I like cooking, and Mom bought a new wok, which is wonderful for stir-frying." She looked curiously at Second Sister. "Do you do any cooking? Since music is so important, you probably don't have much time for anything except practicing."

Second Sister laughed shyly. "Music is important to me, but that doesn't mean I don't enjoy many other things."

"Hey, that's right: You like soccer," said Melanie. "I saw you at the game the other night."

I noticed that Paul was listening intently to the conversation. Did he know that our family had gone because Jason had specifically invited us?

Second Sister seemed anxious to turn the conversation away from the soccer game. "I also enjoy painting," she said. "Brush painting with ink."

Melanie looked excited. "I do, too! On Saturdays, I go to a class on Chinese painting. We also practice writing with a brush."

Second Sister and Melanie started to talk

eagerly about writing with a brush. "How about Paul?" Second Sister asked softly. "Does he practice brush writing, too?"

"Nah," Melanie said. "Scarecrow is only interested in baseball."

"Who is Scarecrow?" I asked. I was confused. One of the entries in Third Sister's notebook of English words defined a scarecrow as a figure made of straw that farmers used to scare away crows.

Melanie laughed. "Scarecrow is my nickname for Paul, because he's scared of crows."

I found it hard to believe that someone as strong and athletic as Paul could be scared of crows. "Is that really true?" I asked him.

He looked embarrassed. "My parents once rented a video called *The Birds*. It's about a town where birds start attacking people. There's a really scary scene with crows. I was little when I saw it, and I've been scared stiff of crows ever since."

"But you're older now," I said. "Didn't you get over it?"

"My *mind* tells me that crows are okay," admitted Paul. "But I still get into a panic when I see one."

Somehow, this made me like him even more. He was still my idol in baseball, but he was also human. How did Second Sister feel, though? Would she look down on Paul for being scared of crows?

Third Sister and I exchanged glances. I saw that she looked unhappy. Her main purpose was getting Second Sister a boyfriend, and that campaign was going nowhere — if you didn't count Jason.

Paul hardly said a word to Second Sister all evening. Instead, he and Eldest Brother began to talk about carpentry, about which saw was best for cutting plywood.

My parents were busy talking to Mr. and Mrs. Eng. They were deeply engrossed in the subject of public schools in America. Third Sister and I were in the outfield, with nobody to talk to.

I decided to concentrate on the food, which was certainly worth it. What if things weren't coming out the way I had expected? At least our family and the Engs were becoming friends.

After that dinner party, it was perfectly natural for me to show up when Paul was out practicing with his team, and he was always glad to see me. Maybe he thought I would be a link between him and Second Sister.

I began to learn a lot from watching the older boys practice. What impressed me most about Paul was his concentration. Only once did I see him distracted, and that was when a crow flew overhead. He struck out.

His teammates got used to seeing me hanging around, and they were pretty patient when I asked them for advice and to explain things.

"Listen," one player said to me, "you've got to make up your mind whether you want to be a home run king or keep your batting average up."

Another said, "Don't forget that Babe Ruth started out life as a scrawny little kid, too."

I didn't need that to remind me that I was a scrawny little kid and might grow up to be a scrawny big kid. Lots of Chinese are small-boned.

Paul saw my face and came over to me. "Hey, don't take it personally. I was pretty scrawny when I was your age." He winked. "Don't worry. Just eat your broccoli and drink plenty of milk."

Paul might not speak Mandarin or know what an *erhu* was, but he had genes similar to mine. If he could hit home runs, I might be able to do it someday, too.

That cheered me up a lot, and I was so pleased that I even began to whistle. That was something Paul did. The trouble was that I couldn't whistle in tune. "Do you have to make that horrible noise?" demanded Second Sister.

Third Sister giggled. "Fourth Brother is whistling because Paul Eng does it."

At the mention of Paul, Second Sister blushed and looked away.

"You admire Paul, don't you?" Eldest Brother asked me.

"Of course I do!" I said. "He's teaching me a lot! I go over to watch him play baseball whenever I can!"

Eldest Brother usually looked at me the same way that I looked at our cat Rita: as someone small to be petted. He never seemed to think of me as somebody who might share his thoughts.

But now Eldest Brother was looking at me as a real person at last. Maybe I was imagining it, but I thought there was a slightly wistful look in his eyes as I described how Paul took time out to give me tips on improving my game.

I soon forgot about Eldest Brother's look.

Second Sister was the one I worried about. What would she do if she learned the truth about our trick?

Third Sister complained that not much seemed to be happening between Paul and Second Sister, but this didn't bother *me*. It was enough that Second Sister had stopped saying insulting things about the Engs. I was also glad that she looked less grouchy these days, although she looked a lot more absentminded.

Mother brought up the subject of inviting the Engs back. "After that wonderful dinner they gave us, we have to have them over to our house," she declared.

Returning hospitality as soon as possible is very important among the Chinese. The problem was that Second Sister and Third Sister were busy most weekend nights with their baby-sitting jobs. Third Sister desperately wanted to go to a summer music camp. Her friend Holly was going to one, and it made Third Sister want to go, too. She was determined to save enough money for the camp this summer, and she baby-sat every chance she got.

Father was playing with the Seattle Symphony most nights. "I'm not playing in the matinee this Saturday," he said. "So I'll be free during the day. We can invite the Engs for lunch."

Mother shook her head. "They invited us to a lavish dinner, and we can't return their hospitality with just a lunch." Lunch is a light meal among the Chinese, and inviting guests for a luncheon is like saying they aren't important enough for a dinner party.

Third Sister had an idea. "How about inviting the Engs for a picnic? Kim was telling me that this is a good time to go into the mountains and see some waterfalls, since we've had all that rain. Their favorite picnic area is at Fern Creek."

Mother considered. It was true that she could include a lot of elegant cold dishes, which would give the meal a higher rating than a lunch. "We don't have a car, though," she said. "Can we get to the Fern Creek picnic grounds by city bus?"

Third Sister's face fell. "I'm afraid not. It's too far out."

"We'll have to hold the picnic in some city park, then," sighed Mother.

"We're the only people I know without a car,"

grumbled Third Sister. She was eager to adopt American ways, and it seemed un-American not to have a car.

Father was too busy to learn to drive. Mother had once been bumped by a taxi in China when she was riding her bike, and after that she wanted nothing to do with anything on wheels. Eldest Brother was old enough to get a license, but he had no interest whatever in learning to drive.

Then I had an idea. "Why don't we ask the Engs to drive us to the picnic?"

Mother was doubtful. "How can we do that? *We* are the ones who are doing the inviting. Besides, there would be ten of us, and we can't possibly all fit in one car!"

"Lots of American families have two cars," said Third Sister. "Some even have three."

"Well, the Engs aren't exactly an American family," said Mother.

"At least call them up and ask," I suggested.

Third Sister and I worked on Mother until she finally picked up the phone.

We heard her mention the idea of a picnic at Fern Creek, and then in a voice thick with embarrassment, she asked if they could possibly drive the whole party to the park.

"Oh, really?" she said finally, and beamed. "How nice of you, Mrs. Eng! I know it's terrible that we have to ask you . . ." She stopped and listened to Mrs. Eng. When she finally hung up, I knew the picnic was on.

7

The day of the picnic was cool, with some unfriendly-looking clouds lurking in the distance. But by the time we set off, the clouds cleared, and we looked forward to a nice day.

Eldest Brother, Father, and I were in Mr. Eng's car with Paul. Mother, Second Sister, Third Sister, and Melanie Eng were in the car driven by Mrs. Eng.

We didn't start out by separating the males from the females. I think everybody became a bit self-conscious when we stood in front of the two cars, trying to decide how to divide the party. We all avoided looking at Second Sister and Paul, who were working hard at not looking at each other.

Finally Mrs. Eng said to her husband with a laugh, "Let's do things the old-fashioned

Chinese way. I'll take the girls, and you take the boys."

I looked at Second Sister, to see if she was disappointed at being in a different car from Paul's. I had the impression that she looked relieved. Then I sneaked a glance at Paul. He also seemed relieved!

Our plot to start a romance between Second Sister and Paul was a flop, apparently. As we got into the two cars, I discovered that *I* was relieved, too. We had become friends with the Eng family without that extra complication.

Since we didn't have a car, our family seldom had a chance to get out of the city. The drive to the Fern Creek picnic grounds took us way out into the countryside at last. I saw some real cows in a field, and then a couple of horses.

"Are we going to see any cowboys today?" I asked Paul excitedly. We Chinese tend to believe that America is filled with cowboys and Indians shooting at each other. When we arrived in Seattle we finally saw some Indians — except that I was told to call them Native Americans. I was awfully disappointed to see that they didn't wear fancy headdresses with feathers. In fact they don't look much different from us Chinese!

"There are no cowboys around here, I'm afraid," said Paul, laughing. "You have to wait until you get to the central or eastern part of Washington State, and even there you won't find too many of them left."

Again I was disappointed. Then I remembered that my friend Matthew had been awfully disappointed when I told him Chinese men didn't wear pigtails anymore, only stubborn girls like Second Sister.

We drove through some mountainous stretches with snow still on them. "Can we climb some of these mountains?" I asked Paul.

He shook his head. "If you mean those hills over there, I'm afraid not. You'd have to be an experienced climber to tackle those. But you can go on one of the trails near the picnic area."

The way he talked about the trails near the picnic area made them sound pretty tame. "Are you an experienced climber?" I asked.

He shrugged. "I'm just so-so. I have friends who are a lot better."

He sounded modest, but I knew he was a good athlete, and I guessed that he was a pretty good climber.

I continued to ask him questions, and soon we were on the subject of baseball. "I'd like to know how you put all that power into your swing," I told him.

Eldest Brother had been silent for most of the trip. Now he suddenly sat up. "That's right — you were asking me about that, Fourth Brother." He turned a puzzled face to Paul. "How is it that you know about swing?"

It wasn't until Eldest Brother mentioned Benny Goodman again that we finally got everything straightened out. Mr. Eng turned around. "Say, my mother was a real fan of Benny Goodman," he said. "According to her, he was one of the greatest clarinetists that ever lived."

Paul grinned at me. "Your brother is talking about swing, a type of music popular in the thirties and forties. He wasn't referring to swinging your bat in baseball."

After that, Eldest Brother sank into his world of music again, and I went back to asking Paul about baseball. I think he enjoyed having someone acting like a younger brother to him. Maybe it was a nice change from having a sister who kept calling him Scarecrow.

The Fern Creek picnic area was fairly far away, but the ride didn't seem long since there was so much to see, even if the scenery didn't look like what I had expected from the movies.

Mrs. Eng drove faster than her husband, and when we arrived at the picnic area, we saw that the others had already found a picnic table. There were some people with them. When we pulled up, I recognized the O'Mearas.

Third Sister and Kim were talking to each other and laughing. "When Kim told me this was a good time for picnics at Fern Creek, I didn't know her family was planning one, too!" cried Third Sister. "Isn't this a great surprise?"

Third Sister might be delighted to see her best friend here, but what about everyone else? Mr. and Mrs. O'Meara were smiling and greeting the Engs, whom they had already met. Jason, however, was standing to one side and examining his shoes.

I stole a glance at Second Sister. She was also examining her shoes. That left Paul. Yes, he was examining his shoes as well.

"Come on, Yinglan!" cried Mother. "What's wrong with you? Help me set the table!"

Second Sister started and looked up. "Yes, Mother," she muttered, and began to help set out the platters of Chinese food.

Mother and my two sisters had really worked hard to prepare food for the picnic. They had cooked beef until it nearly fell apart, and then cooled the meat in its own juices to form a hard jelly, which they sliced. The roast chicken had been chopped into bite-sized pieces. We had a salad of bean sprouts, which both Father and I love, and several rounds of onion bread. Just looking at the food made my mouth fill with saliva.

Our guests, the Engs, seemed eager to start on the food as well, but they weren't the only ones. Mr. O'Meara looked at our table. "Gee, that roast chicken looks good!"

Actually, wonderful smells were also coming from the O'Mearas' barbecue grill. They had a charcoal fire going, and Mr. O'Meara had been grilling hamburgers and salmon steaks.

Mother and Mrs. O'Meara looked at each other and then said almost simultaneously, "Why don't we share our food?"

"Yeah, let's have a potluck!" cried Kim.

So it was decided to join the two parties. Third Sister took out her notebook and asked Kim to explain the word *potluck*. She wanted to know why the pot was lucky.

"Well, it's not the pot," said Kim. "I guess we call the party a potluck because you get something good out of the pot if you're lucky."

So we wound up with a big party of fourteen

people. For a while we were all busy eating and talking, and I forgot about Second Sister and the two boys who were supposed to like her — no, wait — the two boys she was supposed to like — or whatever.

I ate and ate. I had three pieces of chicken, a hamburger, a piece of salmon, and two pieces of onion bread. I almost forgot to eat the bean sprout salad. If you piled together all the food I ate, I bet it would make a ball almost the size of my head. Scary, isn't it?

I wasn't the only hog in the party. By the time Mother and Mrs. O'Meara started clearing away the dishes, some of us were lying on the grass, making little grunts, moans, and urps.

Finally Jason sat up. "Hey, we can't let this gorgeous day go to waste. Who wants to play Hacky Sack?"

He took a small, soft bag out of his pocket, about the size of a muffin. Then he kicked it into the air with the side of his foot and kept it in the air by kicking, without once letting the little sack fall to the ground.

I immediately recognized it as a Chinese game called *tijuanzi*. Second Sister went up to him. "Not bad," she said.

Jason kicked the sack toward her, and she

caught it neatly with her foot and kicked it back to him. After they kept this up for a while, Second Sister began to do some tricks, such as twirling around between kicks.

Kim joined in, and Second Sister kicked the sack to her. Kim tried the trick of spinning between kicks, but the sack fell on the ground.

"You're pretty good," Second Sister told Jason. "You must play a lot."

"Yeah, it really helps my footwork in soccer, too," said Jason.

"Actually, it's played mostly by girls in China," said Second Sister. "My grandmother used to be a champion at it. She said in the old days even women with bound feet became real experts."

Jason looked crushed. Then he smiled rue-fully. "Oh, well. I don't care. I enjoy the game, whatever people think."

I found myself admiring Jason. I had never liked him before, but now I began to respect him for not caring what other people thought.

Jason and Second Sister started to kick the sack again, and pretty soon Melanie Eng and Third Sister also wanted to play. There was a lot of laughter and good-natured kidding.

Suddenly I realized that Paul wasn't one of

the players. I looked around and finally saw him standing off to one side, under some cedar trees. He had a dark scowl on his face.

I had forgotten all about the rivalry — the phony rivalry — between Jason and Paul. What would Paul do? Would he join the Hacky Sack game?

He had probably never played it before. Otherwise why would he be standing under a tree, scowling?

After a while the Hacky Sack players stopped and plopped down on the ground, laughing and panting. "Can I get you something to drink?" Jason asked Second Sister. "We've got cans of pop in the ice chest."

As Jason and Second Sister sat on the grass sipping their drinks, Paul suddenly stepped forward. "Say, it's such a nice day! Who wants to go on a hike to Walton Falls?"

The grown-ups all said they were happy just sitting around in the forest, chatting and enjoying the scenery.

Melanie and Kim were busy trying to explain an Easter egg hunt to Third Sister, who was having a hard time understanding how a bunny could lay eggs.

At Paul's question, Melanie shook her head. "I think I'll sit this one out, Scarecrow." She turned to Kim and Third Sister. "How about you?"

Both Third Sister and Kim decided that chocolate Easter eggs were more interesting than waterfalls.

"What about the rest of you?" asked Paul. Although he was looking at me and Third Sister, I knew that he was really talking to Jason and Second Sister.

"I'd love to go," Second Sister said eagerly, getting up. "I like painting waterfalls, but I haven't seen one since I left China."

"After all the rain we've had, I guarantee that we'll see a good one," said Paul.

Jason sprang up from the ground in a single smooth motion. "Sure! I'd like to see the falls, too!"

The two boys stood on either side of Second Sister. They were about the same height. Paul had wider shoulders from swinging his bat, but I knew that Jason was a pretty good athlete, too.

This was beginning to look like a contest between the two boys. It might turn ugly. "I'd like to see the falls, too," I said, jumping up.

So the four of us set out for the trail to Walton
Falls, with Paul in the lead, followed closely —
very closely — by Jason. Then came Second Sister, while I was in the rear.

Paul set a fast pace, and Jason kept up with him
every millimeter of the way. After a while the trail
started to go up steeply, and Second Sister was
soon falling behind. "Tell them to wait for me at
the falls, Fourth Brother," she panted. "This isn't
supposed to be a race!"

I hurried after the two boys, and I was soon

panting, too. "Hey, wait!" I shouted when I got closer. "My sister says she can't keep up!"

They heard me, and to my relief they both stopped. When I caught up with them, Paul asked, "Is Yinglan okay?"

I caught my breath. "She's fine, but she can't go as fast as you two. She said to tell you this isn't a race."

It was exactly the wrong thing to say. At the

word *race*, Paul and Jason looked at each other. I saw the same smile on both their faces, and it wasn't a friendly one.

"Let's see who gets to the falls first," said Jason. "I know a good shortcut."

"I know a good shortcut, too," said Paul.

In the next instant, both of them took off from the trail and started scrambling through the undergrowth.

"Hey, you said to stick to the trail!" I shouted after Paul.

"That's only for inexperienced kids," came Paul's voice, already receding into the distance. Caught up in the rivalry with Jason, Paul no longer sounded like a friendly elder brother.

I was still looking after them when Second Sister caught up with me. "What's happened? Where are the others?"

"They took a shortcut," I said.

Second Sister shook her head at the puzzling behavior of males, and we went on. Soon we began to hear the sound of rushing water. Turning a corner, we arrived finally at the bottom of the falls. Silently we stood and stared in awe at the raging white torrent.

After a while we looked around for Paul and Jason. There was no sign of either one. I asked some people standing by the falls whether they had seen a couple of teenage boys. But they said they hadn't. One woman said that she had been there for almost half an hour and hadn't seen any sign of the boys.

"Strange," murmured Second Sister. She turned slowly and stared at me. "You said the boys were taking a shortcut. Did they explain why?"

"They were racing to see who would reach the falls first," I said weakly.

Second Sister frowned. "That's stupid! Why would they want to do that? It's dangerous to run on these trails. There's still a lot of snow!"

"They wanted to impress you," I mumbled.

Second Sister's mouth dropped open. Finally she closed her mouth with a click. "I can't imagine why they'd do that..." She stopped and blushed. "That is, I think Paul might want to..." Again she stopped in confusion. Then she stared at me again. "But why on earth should *Jason* go racing up the mountain?"

Now it was *my* turn to look down in confusion. "Jason thinks you like him, so he feels he should...uh..."

"But why on earth should *Jason* think I like

him?" asked Second Sister. "It's true that I admire the way he plays soccer." She stopped, and then said slowly, "That's right — he invited us to go watch him play. Now, why did he do that?"

There was no way to avoid an answer. "Because he overheard us talking . . . ," I mumbled. I stopped as my tongue became too thick and clumsy. Even with the roaring waterfall, I could hear the pounding of my heart.

Second Sister's eyes narrowed.

8

"You wanted Jason to overhear you!" snarled Second Sister. "I see it now! It was a plot! And that night, when you and Third Sister were washing dishes, you were also planning to be overheard!"

Several seconds passed. Only they felt like several years. Second Sister took a deep breath and said in a thin voice, "What you said about Paul liking me, that was all a lie, too, wasn't it?"

More than anything, I longed to have Third Sister's support at that moment. Together, the two of us could face anything. But Third Sister was down at the picnic area with Kim, and I had to face this blazing fury alone.

It was only right. *I* was the one who had thought of using the idea from the movie. *I* was the one who had suggested having Second Sister and Paul overhear our conversations.

Second Sister's face was yellowish white, like old ivory. She looked like the White Serpent Demon, ready to sink her fangs into my neck. I backed away from her, and slipped and fell on some rotting leaves.

Second Sister loomed over me. "Now tell me why you and Third Sister played this trick on me!" she hissed.

The ground under me was wet and cold, but I didn't try to get up. It felt safer to stay down there. I gulped and tried to find words. "I wanted our family to be friends with the Engs because I hoped Paul would help me with baseball." My voice had become a croak. I struggled on. "But you were always making fun of him and jeering at him for not being able to read and write Chinese. So we thought if we made you think he liked you, you might be nicer to him."

Behind us the waterfall roared. My backside became colder and wetter. I finally found the courage to look up at Second Sister.

Her face had an expression that I don't often see. Since coming to America, Second Sister had mostly looked sad or exasperated. Occasionally she had looked at me with pity, when I played my violin. It took me a while to recognize her expression now: It was shame.

The long silence stretched on and on. I finally decided to risk getting up. Second Sister held out her hand to help me up.

"But why did you include Jason in your trick?" she demanded as she tried to wipe some of the mud from my back.

"Jason was just an accident," I said, not looking at her. "He happened to overhear us when we were rehearsing our talk in the O'Mearas' kitchen."

There was another long silence. Standing there shivering and chilled to the bone, I finally saw how shabby our trick was. No one should try to embarrass somebody else like that. And our victim wasn't just Second Sister: We had also made fools of Paul and Jason.

I finally stole a look at Second Sister. She was trembling all over. Was it from anger, or was it from the cold? Or was she weeping with mortification? Little gasps escaped from her throat, and she was hunched over with pain.

I was alarmed. "Are you all right, Second Sister?"

She made some more *hoo-hoo* noises and shook harder. Suddenly she exploded. Her laughter rang above the waterfall and echoed from the mountainside around us.

A huge wave of relief swept over me. All the tension of the last few weeks relaxed, and I felt my insides wobble. The wobbling turned to spasms, and the spasms turned into gusts of laughter. I laughed so hard that I slid back down again to the wet ground.

Second Sister recovered first. Again she reached down and helped me up.

Suddenly I knew that I loved Second Sister as much as Third Sister, but in a different way. Third Sister is my partner and my ally. Second Sister will always frighten me a little. She can be very harsh sometimes. But she is harsh to herself, too. She has a kind of nobility — what we call *da qi* in Chinese, literally "big breath." She was big enough to forgive me, in spite of the trick I had played on her.

Second Sister sighed. "You were right: I was mean, and there was no excuse for the way I talked about Paul."

We were both shivering with cold now. Second Sister hunched her shoulders and looked around impatiently. "Where can those boys be? They should have arrived before we did. They went faster, and they took shortcuts."

"They also took chances," I said. I began to shiver harder, and not just with cold.

"Maybe they got tired of waiting for us and decided to go back to the picnic area," Second Sister said. She didn't look convinced, however.

"We'd better tell the others what happened," I said.

When we got back, we found neither Paul nor Jason at the picnic area. Mr. Eng was shocked when we told him about the two boys going off the trail and taking shortcuts. "It's not like Paul to take chances! He's not a boy who likes to show off. I wonder what possessed him."

I knew what had possessed him, and Jason, too. When I caught Third Sister's eye, she came up to me and whispered. "What happened?"

"I had to tell Second Sister the truth about our trick," I said.

Third Sister choked. "What did she do to you?" she gasped. "You're still alive and breathing, so she couldn't have been too bad."

"It was pretty scary," I confessed. "Actually she took it better than I expected — better than we deserve. We wound up laughing about it."

Third Sister looked astounded. "I can't believe it! Is Second Sister actually getting soft?"

Suddenly I realized that there was silence in our picnic area. We looked around at the others, and saw that they were all staring at the two of us — except Kim, who was busy studying her shoes.

Father beckoned to us and said in his sternest Chinese-father-who-must-be-obeyed voice, "Yingmei! Yingtao! Come here!"

Third Sister and I shuffled over to him. I stole a glance at Mother. Her face was every bit as stern.

"Is this true?" demanded Father. "Did you two plan this cruel trick on your sister?"

Second Sister actually defended us. "I don't think their intention was to be cruel, exactly," she murmured.

Third Sister was blinking back tears. "Second Sister was lonely here in America because she had to leave all her friends in China," she said, snuffling. "So I thought we'd arrange for her to become friends with Paul. Jason was just an accident."

We looked over to the O'Mearas. Mr. and Mrs. O'Meara were apparently having some stern words with Kim.

Finally Father walked over to the Engs, who

were looking completely bewildered by everything. All except Melanie Eng. She had been at the Science Center, where we had staged the conversation overheard by Paul. He had told her about Second Sister having a crush on him. She looked over at us and gave us a big wink.

"I'm sorry, Mr. Eng," said Father. He was having trouble getting his words out. "These two children have played an unforgivable trick on your son. They made him think that Yinglan secretly admired him."

Mr. and Mrs. Eng looked acutely uncomfortable. After some seconds, Mrs. Eng coughed. "We did wonder. Up to now, Paul's always been terribly bashful with girls."

"Even if their attraction is not a real one," added Mr. Eng, "I hope it doesn't affect the friendship between our families."

"Personally I think this is a broadening experience for Paul," added Melanie.

Mr. O'Meara, who had approached, grinned at Melanie's remark. "And for Jason, too. That kid's whole life consisted of soccer. At least he knows that girls exist now."

"Anyway, there's no harm done," said Mrs. O'Meara.

"I'm not so sure," said Second Sister slowly.

"Paul and Jason didn't arrive at the falls. We don't know what's happened to them."

Mr. O'Meara's grin faded. "How long have they been gone?"

Second Sister looked at me. "What do you think, Fourth Brother? We started up the trail at about two o'clock."

"Paul and Jason went off the trail about a quarter of an hour later," I said.

Mr. O'Meara consulted his watch. "So the boys have been gone almost two hours."

"It shouldn't take them that long to reach the falls," said Mrs. O'Meara. "Dear God, they must have got lost!"

It was out in the open now. Mrs. O'Meara had expressed the fear we all felt.

Mr. Eng tried to be reassuring. "They can't have wandered too far off. All they have to do is keep going up, and they're bound to hit the highway."

"Maybe they hit the highway a couple of miles up the road," suggested Mr. O'Meara. "Why don't I drive along the highway and see if I can spot the boys? They could be waiting by the side of the road."

"I bet they're feeling pretty foolish right now," said Mrs. O'Meara.

"They certainly deserve to feel foolish!" said Mr. Eng. "What a stupid thing, that race! I thought Paul would have more sense!"

"I think I'll go back up the trail again," I said. "Maybe they found their way back to the trail."

The grown-ups were still convinced that Paul and Jason were somewhere higher up the mountain, and they ignored my suggestion. In fact they made a point of ignoring me completely. Mr. Eng and Mr. O'Meara drove off in their cars, and the others decided to wait at the picnic area, in case the boys came back.

Feeling like an outcast, I made my way to the trailhead. There were steps behind me. I was joined by two other outcasts, Third Sister and Kim.

"Do you think we'll find them soon?" asked Third Sister. Her voice was trembling a little.

"We'd better," said Kim. "It can get pretty cold up here in the mountains. If we don't find them by evening, they're in real danger of hypothermia."

I didn't know what *hypothermia* meant, but I could guess. "It's all my fault," I said miserably.

"No, you can't blame yourself for everything," said a voice behind me. It was Eldest

Brother. "The boys were experienced enough to know that it was a bad idea to leave the trail."

Just when I think that Eldest Brother has no room in his mind for anything but music, he comes out with something steady and comforting. At times like these I'm glad he's my brother, after all. "I'll help you look for them," he offered.

"No, we should do it ourselves," Third Sister said stubbornly. "The three of us started this whole thing, and we have to be the ones to do the searching."

We left Eldest Brother standing by the trailhead. He looked a bit lonely, somehow.

The trail was muddy, and in places we could make out footprints. We finally came to the place where the larger ones stopped. I called out to Kim and Third Sister. "I think this is where Jason and Paul went off on their shortcuts."

The bushes showed a break, and we peered through. Kim shook her head in disbelief. "I still can't believe that Jason would do something stupid like this!"

I had to defend my baseball idol. "Paul isn't stupid, either!"

"They were both stupid," sighed Third Sister. "And so were we."

I looked into the bushes again, and I could make out sort of an informal trail, made by passing feet. "Maybe we can try the shortcut ourselves."

Third Sister shook her head. "We might get lost, too."

Suddenly I remembered the story about two kids lost in a forest. Only they didn't really get lost, because they left a trail of bread crumbs behind them. "Do we have any bread crumbs?" I asked.

Third Sister smiled slowly. "You're thinking of that opera we saw last month, aren't you? *Hansel and Gretel?*"

The three of us searched our pockets for something to leave a trail. I had some rubber bands left over from helping my friend Matthew deliver newspapers, and a half-eaten gumdrop covered with lint. Third Sister had her notebook of English words, a pencil with the lead broken off, and a chip from a piece of resin. Kim had a worn-out ticket stub, a photo of some movie star, which she quickly thrust back into her pocket, and a wad of paper tissues.

"We could tear the pages from your notebook into little bits," suggested Kim.

Third Sister clutched the notebook to her chest. "I worked hard to collect these words and phrases!"

"We'll just use the blank pages," Kim said quickly.

So that was what we did: tore Third Sister's notebook paper into thin strips and hung them on branches about every ten steps.

We finally stopped to catch our breath. "I'm running out of blank pages," said Third Sister.

"I've got my baseball cap, and I can take off my socks," I offered.

Kim began to giggle. "We'll be doing striptease: a sock here and a shirt there! If we don't find the boys soon, we'll wind up bare naked!"

We had another problem. At first the passage of the two boys was pretty obvious, but after a while it became harder to make out.

"You know what?" said Kim. "Jason and Paul could have separated somewhere."

She was right. The two boys were racing to reach the falls. Each one must have thought he had a better route.

"Maybe we should separate, too," said Third Sister.

"Even if we start stripping, we barely have enough . . . ," I started to say. I stopped when the two girls giggled.

"We can't afford to separate," I continued, "because we don't have enough stuff to mark *two* trails."

Kim and Third Sister had to agree, so the three of us slogged on together. "I hope they didn't get into a fight or something," Third Sister said worriedly.

"Paul wouldn't get into a fight over a girl!" I said.

"I certainly can't imagine Jason fighting over anything except soccer," said Kim.

"Hey, maybe we can try yelling," I suggested. I was so frustrated that I *felt* like yelling.

"Okay, let's yell in unison," said Third Sister. She raised her arms like a conductor. "A one, a two . . ." And we yelled together as loud as we could, "Jason! Paul!"

The echo of our yell bounced back at us. Then silence. We waited. But we heard nothing.

Kim sighed. "It's hopeless. We'd better go back, or our parents will start worrying about *us* next."

"Maybe the boys are back at the picnic area by now," said Third Sister.

116

We turned around and started back down. Suddenly I stopped. "Let's try once more, at least."

"Okay," said Third Sister. "What have we got to lose, except our voices? Maybe we should yell at a higher pitch. It carries better."

So we gave a higher yell, a bloodcurdling scream. Even the echo sounded gruesome.

We waited. Nothing. Kim sighed again. "Okay, guys, let's go."

"Wait, what was that?" said Third Sister. She has good ears. "I think I hear something," she said.

We stood and listened hard. Finally I heard a faint shout, but it came from below instead of above.

"Let's yell again," said Third Sister, and raised her arms to conduct us. Encouraged, we yelled even louder, "Jason! Paul!"

This time, the answering shout was unmistakable.

"They really got lost!" said Kim. "Instead of going *up* to the falls, they went *down!*"

We headed for the direction where the shout had come from. We had run out of notebook paper, so we began to tear up Kim's wad of tissues for markers. Every now and then, we yelled again, to check that we were going in the right direction. My throat was starting to hurt.

"Why don't the boys come over?" asked Kim. "We're doing all the work."

Before I could say anything, Third Sister said it for me. "Maybe one of them is hurt."

At least the answering shouts grew louder, which meant we were getting closer. Third Sister saw them first. "There they are!"

We found Paul and Jason in a gully, which was slippery and wet. They were both sitting hunched over on the ground. They were scratched and muddy, and their faces were drawn. Even more alarming, they didn't get up when they saw us.

We rushed forward. "What happened?" cried Kim.

Paul seemed to be in pain, but he tried to grin. "I was climbing pretty fast, and I thought I'd beat Jason easily. Then I...uh..." He stopped.

I guessed what had happened. "You saw a crow!"

He nodded, looking very embarrassed. "A crow flew over me, and I was so rattled that I slipped and went slithering downhill. I hit bottom real hard and felt my ankle go." He turned and looked at Jason. "It's your story now."

"When I heard Paul slide down the hill, I thought I'd win the race for sure," Jason began. "Then I heard him give a grunt, and I knew something had happened to him."

Paul took over. "He could have left me here and kept on going to win the race. Instead, he came down to see how I was doing and —"

Jason finished the sentence. "I slipped and came tumbling down like a ton of bricks. So here we are, both with busted ankles. Boy, do I feel like an idiot!"

"No, you're not an idiot!" Kim cried warmly. "I'm proud of you, Jason!"

It had been generous of Jason to come down to find out what had happened to Paul. I found myself liking him a lot more.

Then Paul and Jason turned and stared at the three of us. It was like being drilled by laser beams.

"Since we've been down here, we've had lots of time to talk," Paul said. His voice was soft but menacing. "We started to compare notes."

He paused, and the silence became heavy.

"S-so wh-what sort of notes did you two c-compare?" Third Sister finally asked in a husky little voice.

Jason answered. "We compared certain little conversations we overheard, concerning your sister. Apparently she has a crush on both of us. A bit hard to believe, isn't it?"

I was quaking, but even together, Paul and Jason frightened me less than Second Sister by herself. Besides, they had sprained ankles and couldn't run after us.

"So you set us up?" demanded Jason. "The three of you got together and plotted to make us look stupid?"

"I haven't done anything to deserve this!" cried Paul. "Why did you do this to me? To us?"

As usual, Third Sister was the one who explained. "My sister was lonely and didn't have any friends in America. So we tried to arrange a boyfriend for her."

"My God, I see it now," Paul whispered. "You used the trick from *Much Ado about Nothing!*" It seemed he had seen the same movie. "This means Yinglan thought I had a crush on *her!*" He stopped and whistled. "Boy, is she going to be livid when she learns the truth!"

"She already knows," I muttered. "I had to

tell her everything, to explain why the two of you were racing up to the falls."

"But why did you have to involve *both* of us?" asked Jason. "Was it because you wanted a spare, in case it didn't work with Paul?"

Like Paul, Jason didn't seem quite so angry anymore. Kim got up the courage to answer. "You were just an accident, Jason."

So we had to explain everything. At the end, Paul's lips were twitching. Jason started to laugh but winced instead.

"We've got to get out of here," said Paul. Both he and Jason were thoroughly wet and were in pain. From the looks of things they had tried to drag themselves up from the gully but hadn't got very far.

"Say, how did you guys find us, anyway?" asked Jason. "I sure hope you aren't lost, too."

We told them about the paper trail we had left. Paul laughed. "First we were set up by some characters from *Much Ado about Nothing*, and now we're rescued by *Hansel and Gretel!* We'd better get out of these woods before we meet Snow White and the Seven Dwarfs!"

9

The next morning, Third Sister and I were up first, as usual. Second Sister came down as we were preparing our Sunday breakfast of eggs fried with rice. On weekends she normally sleeps as late as she can. I suspected that she came down early because she wanted to talk to us before the others were up.

"I still don't understand why you went to all that trouble to arrange a boyfriend for me," she said, helping herself to some of our fried rice.

"We knew how much you missed your old friends," said Third Sister. "We thought if you had a boyfriend here in America, you wouldn't miss China so much."

"How very kind of you!" said Second Sister, with some of her old sarcasm. "But why did the friend have to be a *boy?* Since you obviously feel that I'm incapable of making my own friends, why didn't you supply a girl?"

We had no answer to that. The idea was from the movie, and we had simply followed the plot. Finally Third Sister said, "Well, you're fifteen years old already, and at that age kids are starting to date."

"Is that right?" said Second Sister. Now her voice was really cutting. "You're expecting me to start dating because I'm fifteen. In China we don't start dating until we're much older! Well, I don't feel ready to date boys yet. We can't do something just because people expect us to!"

"Then what about Paul?" I said. "*He* can't behave like a perfect Chinese just because you expect him to!"

"Why shouldn't he?" demanded Second Sister. "That's what he is: Chinese."

"He isn't Chinese," I said. "He's American."

After a moment Second Sister said, "He's *Chinese-American.*"

I've heard people here called Chinese-American, Japanese-American, Native American, and so on. But this is unfair. We Yangs are truly Chinese-American, because we live in America but still feel Chinese — even Third Sister.

"Paul is as American as Jason," I said.

"He *looks* completely Chinese," said Second Sister. "Or is he planning to dye his hair blond, the way some Asian kids do?"

"Maybe those kids are just doing it to make their parents mad," said Third Sister. "I've seen punks with green or purple hair."

"I don't see any *Asian* kids with green or purple hair," retorted Second Sister. "They dye it blond because they want to look American. It's pathetic! Why can't they be proud of their natural looks?"

I thought about our own family. Second Sister stayed completely Chinese, while Third Sister tried to be American. At least she never dyed her hair blond. "We Yangs still remember how to be Chinese because we haven't been here very long," I said finally. "But Paul was *born* here. The only country he knows is America."

"Then it's the duty of his parents to teach him about his own country," said Second Sister.

"Paul's own country is America," Third Sister said softly. "The same as Jason's. The O'Mearas' ancestors originally came from Ireland, but you don't call Jason or Kim Irish-American, do you?"

I helped myself to the last of the fried rice. "Why do we have to give everybody a label, anyway?"

"Everybody has to be *something*," Second Sister said stubbornly. "You can't deny your heritage."

Again she was talking about heritage — something you inherit. Was it nationality? Black hair? A good ear for music? I certainly didn't inherit the Yang family gift for music.

I guess the three of us will always disagree. Second Sister believes that if you have black hair and sallow skin and Asian eyes, then you should act like an Asian because that's your heritage.

Third Sister believes that since we're living in America, we should act like Americans.

I believe people should just be themselves, not what other people expect them to be. Not all Americans are cowboys; not all Chinese wear pigtails — just stubborn girls like Second Sister.

People don't always behave the way you expect them to. After the picnic, Paul and Jason became friends, although they didn't seem to have anything in common at all. What was even more surprising was that they sometimes included Second Sister when they went out. I saw them drive up once and pick up Second Sister, and the three of them looked relaxed and cheerful. Instead of staring at their shoes, they stood and chatted pleasantly without any embarrassment. I guess it helped that nobody had a crush on anybody.

One Saturday, Jason called and said that he and Paul were going to a new Disney movie that everybody was wild to see. They were planning on taking Kim, so would my sisters and I like to go with them?

I should have been suspicious of their generosity. In fact I asked Paul outright why he was being so nice to us, considering the trick we played on him.

He laughed. "I owe you one. My fall shocked me out of my fear of crows! So one good thing came out of that picnic, anyhow."

In the end. I accepted the invitation because I was eager to see the movie. My two sisters accepted, too.

The movie was as exciting as the ads said it would be, but I found it very scary in places — although I'd die rather than admit it. When we came out of the auditorium, Jason went off to get the car. The rest of us waited just inside the lobby, since it was raining hard. Third Sister and Kim were talking about the movie. I looked around and saw that Second Sister and Paul had their heads together, talking very earnestly. They seemed to have forgotten us completely.

I nudged Third Sister and pointed. "You think Second Sister and Paul are interested in each other, after all?" I whispered.

"Let's try to find out," she whispered back. She passed my nudge on to Kim, who didn't need any explanation.

Second Sister and Paul were standing conveniently near the telephone stand. The three of us were able to position ourselves behind the stand, out of sight but not out of hearing.

"I've got lots of money saved from baby-sitting," Second Sister was saying. "By the end of the school year there should be enough to send Fourth Brother to the camp. My parents also agree that this is the best thing for him."

"But are you sure he wants to go to a music camp?" asked Paul. "He loves baseball, and I was hoping to help him with his batting this summer."

"The camp will help him realize his potential

as a violinist," Second Sister said firmly. "His problem was not concentrating hard enough."

I felt my blood turning to ice. Second Sister had never accepted the fact that I had a terrible ear for music. To her, a good ear was part of the Yang family heritage.

"I guess Mary and Kim can help him, too," murmured Paul.

I felt a violent shudder from Third Sister standing beside me. She had her heart set on the summer music camp, and had worked hard to save money for it. Both she and Kim had looked forward to the camp for months. Now she would be stuck with a younger brother with a terrible ear for music! I looked over at Kim and saw that her eyes were also wide with horror. She would share Third Sister's disgrace, since the two of them were good friends.

There was a beep outside: Jason had pulled up to the curb with the car. We saw Second Sister and Paul hurry out, and we numbly followed.

The ride back was a silent one, as the three of us in the backseat tried to digest the horrible news.

When the car pulled up at our house, Third Sister and I crawled miserably out. I heard laughter behind me and spun around to look at Second Sister.

Then I saw that both Paul and Jason were laughing also.

Third Sister and I exchanged glances. We finally realized what had happened. Better than anybody, we should have known that you can't always believe what you hear from eavesdropping!

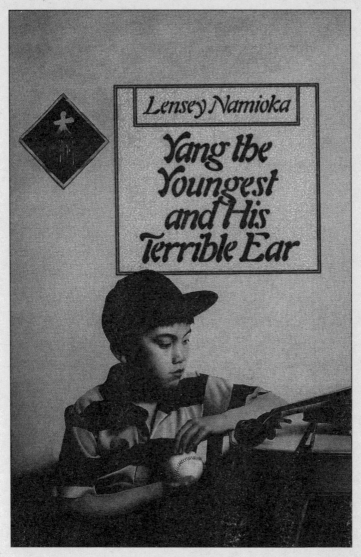

"You know, you're really lucky!" Matthew said suddenly.

I was surprised. "You're the one who's lucky. You're musical. My brother says so, and so does my father."

"But at *your* house, people are happy when you make music," Matthew said in a low voice. "At *my* house, people say, 'Oh, not that again!' when I play my violin."

"At my house, people are *not* happy when I make music," I said. "People say, 'Oh, not that again!' when *I'm* the one who is playing the violin."

We looked at each other. "Too bad we can't trade places," sighed Matthew.

That was when I had my brilliant idea. "Maybe," I said slowly, "we can."

And here's another Yearling about the Yang family!

Lensey Namioka

Yang the Third and Her Impossible Family

The companion to
Yang the
Youngest
and
His Terrible
Ear

Illustrated by Kees de Kiefte

0-440-41231-5

Suddenly Kim didn't seem so friendly any more. Jason was Kim's elder brother, and I began to suspect that he was one of the boys who had taunted Eldest Brother and tripped him.

I began to tremble with anger and got up abruptly. "Excuse me, I see someone over there I have to talk to."

I joined some girls who were jumping rope and tried to stop thinking about the hateful things Kim had said. Earlier, I had thought that I might even get to be friends with her. She could be really funny sometimes, and I liked the way she rolled her eyes, inviting everyone to laugh along with her.

She was probably jealous of me because I was becoming better friends with Holly. I had to be careful and make sure she didn't turn Holly against me. Also, she might tell Jason about the kitten, and the news could reach Eldest Brother. From now on, Kim was the enemy.